Argentum

PRAISE FOR *STORYSHARES*

"One of the brightest innovators and game-changers in the education industry."
– Forbes

"Your success in applying research-validated practices to promote literacy serves as a valuable model for other organizations seeking to create evidence-based literacy programs."

- Library of Congress

"We need powerful social and educational innovation, and Storyshares is breaking new ground. The organization addresses critical problems facing our students and teachers. I am excited about the strategies it brings to the collective work of making sure every student has an equal chance in life."
– Teach For America

"Around the world, this is one of the up-and-coming trailblazers changing the landscape of literacy and education."
- International Literacy Association

"It's the perfect idea. There's really nothing like this. I mean wow, this will be a wonderful experience for young people."   - Andrea Davis Pinkney, Executive Director, Scholastic

"Reading for meaning opens opportunities for a lifetime of learning. Providing emerging readers with engaging texts that are designed to offer both challenges and support for each individual will improve their lives for years to come. Storyshares is a wonderful start."
- David Rose, Co-founder of CAST & UDL

Argentum

Abigail Mitchell

STORYSHARES

Story Share, Inc.
New York. Boston. Philadelphia

Storyshares
Story Share, Inc.
24 N. Bryn Mawr Avenue #340
Bryn Mawr, PA 19010-3304
www.storyshares.org

Inspiring reading with a new kind of book.

Interest Level: High School
Grade Level Equivalent: 5.9

9781642611328

Book design by Storyshares

Printed in the United States of America

Storyshares Presents

1

All across Lirana, faces turned to the broad, white sky as wind rippled across the hills and fields in a large gust. Babies ceased their crying and stared in wonderment, and young and old alike stopped what they were doing to drop their heads in prayer.

Magic weaved its way across the land in silver streaks, blurring across the sky in glowing knots. In temples and shrines across the land, locked boxes were opened and parcels taken out, half-remembered prayers spilling from withered lips.

"A girl," they whispered. "A daughter has been granted, glory be. The curse may finally be gone!"

And as the people celebrated, a tiny newborn with a tuft of downy white hair was wrapped in a soft white cloth and placed into her mother's arms. An exhausted smile rested on her face as she stroked her baby's cheek, clueless to the magic weaving itself around her daughter.

In the other room, her husband sat with his head in his hands as the midwife delivered the decree that sealed his fate.

"A daughter has been born to you, my lord. What do you want done with her?"

He looked up at the woman who had delivered his father and grandfather, with her mother before her doing the same service for his family. "What should be done?"

The woman lifted her shoulders and took an amulet from her neck. "I will give the child this," she said solemnly. "It will protect her for the first fifteen years of her life. Afterwards, I cannot say. Your family's curse is a dark and knotted thing, not even my magic can stop it all. Perhaps it can be undone, but until then, you must prepare for the worst."

He nodded and pressed two golden coins into her hand as he took the necklace. It was so small, barely the size of his little finger, a dull purple stone on a silver cord that gave off a faint silvery glow.

This was nothing new; the same gift had been bestowed to each girl in his family since they could remember, and they each died. He hoped beyond hope that his child would live, that perhaps the curse that had plagued his family for generations would finally, finally end, but until his daughter was grown, he would know no peace.

Quietly, he made his way to where his wife and child lay, staring down at their sleeping forms with love and sadness, pride and fear.

The child opened her clear blue eyes and whimpered softly. In a moment, she was in his arms, her warm, soft body tucked against his chest.

"It will all be fine, my sweet girl. My sweet Selene," he murmured, rubbing her back as she drifted back to sleep. "I will always protect you."

2

Fifteen years passed, and Selene grew up knowing only the castle and the enclosed gardens in which she'd been born, encased in a protective charm by the amulet laced around her neck. The magic that had been woven around her thrummed in time to her heart, and as she grew with the warnings of her parents soaking her mind, she became willful and headstrong, unharmed by anything with the amulet's protection.

As she neared the day when the magic surrounding her would end and the tragedies that had befallen her father's family for centuries would fall upon her too, her father grew more frantic and anxious that something be done to stop it. And so, as the day crept closer, her father made a decision. He issued a challenge to all the knights, wizards, and anyone brave enough and willing enough to take on a quest that may well cost them their lives.

Within a fortnight, there were twenty men and half as many women lined up in the courtyard awaiting the chance to prove their worth. The day arrived when they were to be sent on their mission, and Selene begged to be allowed to go as one of the hopefuls for the hundredth time.

"Father," she pleaded, clutching at his coat. "Please, allow me to try. I want to be the one to undo my curse. It's the only thing I've ever wanted. Please, Father."

"Selene, you cannot," he began, intending to put it to rest once and for all, when her words stopped him cold.

"Whether or not I go, I'm likely to die anyway. Within a month, this charm will end and I'll be open to the curse like your sister and the others before her. If I go, I at least have the chance to control my own fate. Please, please, let me try." She looked up at him, blue eyes shining with determination, and he was powerless against her.

Looking away, he nodded, and she wrapped her arms around him, pressing her face to his chest.

"I love you, Father."

"And I love you, my dear. I will allow you to go, but on one condition." He waited until she acknowledged him, then said, "You must choose one of them to take with you. If the worst happens, I want you..." He hesitated. "I want you to be as safe as possible. Who you take is your choice."

"Of course, Father." She smiled, and it was like the sun breaking through the clouds. "I'll meet you in the courtyard in a moment, I just need to change and pack a bag."

She turned and ran down the corridor, skirt flapping at her ankles, and he stared after her for a moment. He found himself mouthing the words of the prayer his parents had taught him to protect his loved ones from harm. Now, he could only hope that a way was found to undo the curse before the end of the month, or else the daughter he held dear above all else would soon be a memory.

3

Fifteen years passed, and Selene grew up knowing only the castle and the enclosed gardens in which she'd been born, encased in a protective charm by the amulet laced around her neck. The magic that had been woven around her thrummed in time to her heart, and as she grew with the warnings of her parents soaking her mind, she became willful and headstrong, unharmed by anything with the amulet's protection.

As she neared the day when the magic surrounding her would end and the tragedies that had befallen her father's family for centuries would fall upon her too, her father grew more frantic and anxious that something be done to stop it. And so, as the day crept closer, her father made a decision. He issued a challenge to all the knights, wizards, and anyone brave enough and willing enough to take on a quest that may well cost them their lives.

Within a fortnight, there were twenty men and half as many women lined up in the courtyard awaiting the chance to prove their worth. The day arrived when they were to be sent on their mission, and Selene begged to be allowed to go as one of the hopefuls for the hundredth time.

"Father," she pleaded, clutching at his coat. "Please, allow me to try. I want to be the one to undo my curse. It's the only thing I've ever wanted. Please, Father."

"Selene, you cannot," he began, intending to put it to rest once and for all, when her words stopped him cold.

"Whether or not I go, I'm likely to die anyway. Within a month, this charm will end and I'll be open to the curse like your sister and the others before her. If I go, I at least have the chance to control my own fate. Please, please, let me try." She looked up at him, blue eyes shining with determination, and he was powerless against her.

Looking away, he nodded, and she wrapped her arms around him, pressing her face to his chest.

"I love you, Father."

"And I love you, my dear. I will allow you to go, but on one condition." He waited until she acknowledged him, then said, "You must choose one of them to take with you. If the worst happens, I want you..." He hesitated. "I want you to be as safe as possible. Who you take is your choice."

"Of course, Father." She smiled, and it was like the sun breaking through the clouds. "I'll meet you in the courtyard in a moment, I just need to change and pack a bag."

She turned and ran down the corridor, skirt flapping at her ankles, and he stared after her for a moment. He found himself mouthing the words of the prayer his parents had taught him to protect his loved ones from harm. Now, he could only hope that a way was found to undo the curse before the end of the month, or else the daughter he held dear above all else would soon be a memory.

4

Spira and Selene set out almost immediately, heading toward the border of the city. At the top of the hill, Selene stopped, staring out at the land sprawling before her. The castle she had lived in her entire life stood behind her like a sentinel.

Spira paused and turned to look over her shoulder. "You coming?"

"Yes, just... I've never seen anything so beautiful," Selene admitted.

Spira stared at her and shook her head. "You haven't looked in a mirror before, then, huh? Well, let's get on our way. We've only got a month until the princess keels over."

"Right, right. Sorry." She spurred her horse on, following Spira into the unknown.

"If all goes well, we'll find the nasty piece of work that cast that curse and get it all squared away, then we split the profit. We'll decide on who gets what amount afterwards." She looked at Selene as if daring her to argue. "For now, let's get as far as we can before it gets dark."

They continued, stopping every few hours to rest and scout the area. Within half a day's travel, Selene had already learned how to build a fire and skin small animals, though the guts made her ill.

Spira was surprised that she didn't hurt herself doing either task, grumbling that some people had all the luck.

Selene tried to explain why Spira's callouses and scars were fascinating and special, but the other girl just brushed her off. Lessons continued, with Selene picking up new and exciting skills at every turn.

This travel pattern continued for the first week, until they had their first brush of danger. Half done with the nightly preparations, Spira suddenly hushed Selene's chatter and drew her blade.

"Raiders," she mouthed, gesturing to a spot just outside the firelight.

Almost instantly after being noticed, they sprang into action, and the small clearing exploded into chaos. Spira sprung away, lithe as a cat, and took on two men by herself, her curved blades glinting, and Selene was left on her own against the last one.

Her only thought before he rushed her was, *I've never seen someone so huge,* and then she was on the ground, dirt and other ick pressing into her face, with him pressing down on her back.

Partly aware that this *should* hurt, she squirmed valiantly and managed to wedge her hip just so, and a violent jerk had the man on his side on the ground, wheezing pitifully. She reached into the fire and grabbed a burning log and bashed him over the head with it.

When she turned around, Spira was watching her with a concerned expression, her eyes on the burning wood in Selene's hand.

"Girl, where did you learn that?"

Selene laughed and dropped the log back into the fire. "I have to explain some things."

The night had settled over them by the time Selene explained what was going on and why she didn't get hurt. Spira just kept shaking her head. When Selene asked if Spira still wanted her around, Spira guffawed and slapped her shoulder.

"The way I see it," she explained between bites of rabbit, "is that I don't have to protect you as much. Sorry about that, by the way, Princess." She smirked. "Thanks for telling me *after* you got pummeled. Gives me an easy out about explaining that to your parents."

They talked and laughed for a bit longer, and Selene prepared for sleep. She pulled back her sleeves and rolled up her pant legs, exposing silvery knots spread across her limbs.

"I've been meaning to ask. What is that?" Spira asked, gesturing at the silver, lace-like webbing.

Almost unconsciously, Selene ran her hand over the largest patch, right over her heart.

"This grew when I was little. My mother says I wasn't born with this, but it's a physical manifestation of the amulet's protection. I don't know for sure."

"So how do you know you're cursed? That it wasn't just some freak accident that killed your father's sister?"

"It's been passed down as a story in my family. A witch had been the first love of the first king, and she was jealous that he was going to marry a princess instead of her. She cursed his children and his bloodline. All girls that are born from his direct line die, and there's always a girl child. First or last, doesn't matter. It wouldn't be such a concern for my father if I weren't the only child my parents will have. I'm the last of my father's line, and my mother's too. If I die, there's nothing left."

Spira whistled, pausing in her sharpening to look Selene over. "Those are some mighty heavy issues."

Despite herself, Selene laughed. "I know."

5

A fortnight passed, and Selene found herself waking up every morning surprised... surprised she'd survived another night, certain the magic keeping her alive had given out. She had a week left until what had happened to those before her would happen to her.

She wondered if it was okay for her hands to shake so much.

That night, as they set up camp, Selene collapsed onto her bedding with a hiss, kicking her shoes off. Her feet throbbed, and the sensation was so new that it hurt more than it should.

"Is this what you deal with daily?" she whined, rubbing her feet.

Spira looked at her, vaguely amused. "Oh, Princess, it's a lot worse." Her face suddenly twisted. "Wait. Does this mean your magic is wearing off? Isn't that bad?"

"It's a week away from my birthday," Selene explained tiredly. "We have a week to find the witch and undo this curse, or else the magic is gone and I'll be as vulnerable as anyone else."

Spira whistled, something Selene noticed she did when uncomfortable. "We better get this figured out fast, then. Get some rest, and we'll check out the villager's tips in the morning. First light, okay? Sleep well."

* * *

They'd been walking since dawn, their horses having been left on better ground, traipsing across muddy bogs speckled with hiding rocks and through prickly briars that seemed to go on for miles. Even with the remaining protection of the amulet, the biggest ones cut into Selene's flesh and the rocks snagged her feet and threatened to twist her ankles.

The sun was nearing its highest point when they finally settled on solid ground to plan where they'd go next.

Selene had to blink back tears, thinking about what would happen after the week ended and the magic failed. Yes, other people didn't have magical protections, but other people weren't cursed to die before they could ever see the world.

"You know," Spira said awkwardly, "even if we don't break this curse, I'll protect you while we keep looking. And I'll train you too, so you can properly wield that knife." She took Selene's hand and warmed her cold fingers. "I promise, I'll get you back to your parents safe so you can continue being a pampered princess, and I'll guard you day and night until we get this undone."

Selene nodded, swallowing back tears, and flung her arms around Spira's dark neck. "No matter what, you've become my dearest friend. Thank you."

They parted, and after guzzling down some water and a few pieces of dried fruit, they were on the path again.

Spira was the one who noticed the smoke rising from an out-of-place basin, and she picked the way carefully across the dangerous ground. Selene followed closely after her, matching each of Spira's steps to be sure nothing would go wrong.

They reached the edge of the grassy basin and looked down at a small cottage that seemed to have grown out of the earth and trees.

Twisted limbs sprouted from the roof, boughs weighed down with bright strips of cloth that fluttered in the wind. More ancient trees cluttered the back and side of the cottage. They were spindly, shadowy things that seemed to grasp for the light, seeking to snuff it out. A wide pond stood in the center of the basin, in front of the cottage, ringed about with giant silver orbs on rock pedestals that leaked black and silver smoke and colorful sparks.

Slowly, Selene and Spira picked their way down into the basin, treading quietly. Everything about the place seemed to make Spira uneasy, and anything that could spook the courageous Spira was enough to make Selene wish she was anywhere but there. She looked at her arms, searching for the knot of magic protecting her, and only a faint glimmer lingered, barely noticeable unless she squinted.

They found a hiding spot at the edge of the trees, half-hidden in the inky shadows, and waited for right moment.

6

Time passed slowly, and they were so tense they nearly missed the moment when it came.

A woman hobbled out of the door with a breath-like breeze that whisked across the ground. She was gnarled and bent like an old tree, with a cloud of white hair and milky eyes that seemed to stare through everything around her. Charms and amulets hung from her neck on dozens of cords. They clacked together as she moved, tending to the brightly colored flowers crowding the doorway.

Selene stood slowly, as if pulled out of hiding. "You," she whispered, forgetting the plan, her fingers catching around the amulet she wore.

The witch looked up, eyes lighting on her face. A moment passed in tense silence, the distance between them no longer than a few meters, but still both too long and far too small, and the witch began to laugh.

"The seventh girl of the line, finally come to undo the magic her ancestor had wrought. Tell me, girl, are you a sacrifice come to appease me?"

Resolve straightened Selene's back and she drew the blade Spira had given her. "No," she said. "I'm here to forge my own fate."

Surprise slashed across the witch's face, and she straightened, her gnarled form vanishing like mist in the sun. She was suddenly standing before them as a young woman, as beautiful and terrible as a raging fire. Shadows like ink seemed to drip from the ends of her hair, other creatures more terrible than nightmares writhing in the darkness cast by her gown.

Selene felt Spira's hand brush across hers, the last warm thing she knew before shadows overtook them, stinging cold and as forceful as a winter wind and darker than the deepest pits of the earth. Only the pressure of Spira's fingers against her wrist kept her from falling away into it, and she dragged herself through the pressing darkness, the silver glow of her amulet straining against the darkness.

As suddenly as they had come, the shadows vanished with a rushing noise, and Selene struggled to remain upright as Spira sagged to the ground, her fingers slipping from Selene's. Silver pulsed in Selene's blood, streaking through her veins as the magic that had protected her since birth rallied one last time.

The witch stumbled back a half step, fear growing on her terrible face.

"My fate is mine to create!" Selene yelled, feeling the truth of her words in her soul. "You have no control over my family's line any longer. Your hold over my heritage is gone."

She walked forward, and the witch scuttled back, raising her hands to ward Selene away. "Stay back!"

"You won't be able to hurt anyone again, no matter what slights you perceive from them."

Selene's curved blade went up, and the witch screamed as it descended.

* * *

Selene managed to lift Spira up and carry her into the cottage, where she set her on the bed and arranged the blankets to keep her warm.

As Selene fell back onto the cushions piled against the floor, her amulet glowed brightly one last time. The silver light washed over her and spread over Spira, warm and gentle, before the stone crumbled to pieces, clattering to the floor in dim chunks.

Selene wasn't even aware of the tears on her face until Spira awoke and dropped to her knees in front of her.

"Why are you crying?" Spira asked. "We're alive, aren't we? You defeated the witch... it's all over."

"I know, I don't know why I'm crying. I just... I thought we were on a course for destruction. I didn't ever think... but now..." She sniffed, and Spira wrapped her arms around her.

"We just got to get you home safe, and everything will be okay. Now, does that batty witch have any food here? I'm starving."

Selene managed a giggle. "I didn't check. Maybe some vegetables in the cupboard?"

After putting together a small meal, they set out again, supporting each other as they climbed the basin and began walking out of the bog. As if related to the end of the witch, the path became easier. There were fewer hidden stones, and the ground was firm beneath their feet. The briars seemed to shrink and break off at the slightest brush, and the way was clearer.

They made it back to their horses in half the time, and were once again on their way.

7

A two-week-long journey saw them approaching the city. They had spent the majority of the return conversing quietly about the things they'd seen, carefully skirting the topic that was staring them in the face. Selene didn't want to say goodbye, not when she felt more for Spira than she'd ever known possible.

At the top of the hill where Selene had stopped over a month before, Spira halted. "When this is over," she began. "When... you've gone back to the castle away from all the rest of us, what'll happen?"

"We'll figure it out," Selene promised, hardly knowing herself.

As if steeling herself, Spira took a breath and nodded. "All right. Let's get you home, then, Princess."

* * *

Returning to the city was a grand affair, with music and cheering and confetti swirling in the air. Selene and Spira were led straight into the castle, and Selene was swept up into her parents' arms, tears wetting all their faces.

Spira was thanked over and over again, and she put on airs of being bothered by the whole thing, but her smile told Selene she didn't mind.

A banquet was held, and she and Spira told the story to hundreds of guests, with Selene telling the most of it as Spira tried to slink away. It was late at night, with the dawn not far off, when they both managed to slip away into the courtyard where they'd met.

"Sel," Spira began, fidgeting with her knife handle. "What happens now?"

"What do you mean?" Selene asked, holding her breath.

"I mean," Spira said, looking away, frustrated, "Will I... will I be able to see you again?" She paused and added, "Since I went through all that trouble, and all. I mean, someone still needs to teach you how to use that blade." She pointed at the blade still on Selene's hip. "And it should be me, obviously."

"Spira," Selene said, with both delight and exasperation. "Of course." She watched the relief grow on Spira's face before tacking on, "Now that I'm a frail and delicate flower without a magic amulet, I'll need someone to protect me."

Spira laughed.

Selene laughed too, and linked her arm through Spira's. "Walk with me. I'll show you the gardens."

* * *

Dawn broke over the two as they walked through the flowers hand in hand, enjoying the simple pleasure of company and morning sunlight.

About The Author

Abigail Mitchell was born in Charlottesville, Virginia in 1999, and grew up in Greene County. Ever since a young age, she has loved books, and has enjoyed writing her own. As the youngest of three, she found ways to entertain herself and her family with her stories, often talking nonstop about her newest creations. In middle and high school, with the aid of supportive teachers, friends, and family, she devoted more time to writing. She has competed in NaNoWriMo for several years, and has been working on several works she hopes to publish soon.

After graduating high school, Abigail plans to attend an automotive college and, in her spare time, continue writing in the hopes that more of her work is published.

About The Publisher

Story Shares is a nonprofit focused on supporting the millions of teens and adults who struggle with reading by creating a new shelf in the library specifically for them. The ever-growing collection features content that is compelling and culturally relevant for teens and adults, yet still readable at a range of lower reading levels.

Story Shares generates content by engaging deeply with writers, bringing together a community to create this new kind of book. With more intriguing and approachable stories to choose from, the teens and adults who have fallen behind are improving their skills and beginning to discover the joy of reading. For more information, visit storyshares.org.

Easy to Read. Hard to Put Down.